The Last Caspian Tiger

Zoe Jazz

ISBN: 1-7321335-0-6
ISBN-13: 978-1-7321335-0-1

For my cat,
without whom this story would not exist.

ACKNOWLEDGMENTS

I'd like to thank my friends and family for encouraging and supporting my creativity throughout my life.

I'd also like to thank my co-workers at Semi-Permanent Press for helping me show my work to the world.

1974

Turkey

She sat perched and hidden in the reeds, taking quiet breaths, waiting patiently for the right moment to strike the boar. He drank from the stream greedily, grunting just quiet enough that the birds next to him were undisturbed.

He was unaware of her presence, which made him the perfect prey— an easy, quick kill, dead before it could scream. Her mouth was already watering at the mere thought of his flesh.

She dug her paws into the damp soil, ready to attack.

The boar looked up suddenly, staring towards her. She stayed perfectly still and silent, her nerves on edge. She couldn't be noticed now. Not now.

Still, he stared her way. She didn't know how he could see her through the reeds.

The boar turned and ran.

She leapt out of the foliage, her roar scaring off the birds as she lunged for the boar. The birds leapt towards the clouds, flapping their wings frantically to escape. Her teeth sunk into the back of the boar's neck. His screams rang out as feathers fell from the sky.

He couldn't escape her, though he thrashed against her. Her claws dug into his skin. His body would soon be her feast.

But something was wrong.

As her claws ran down his sides, she did not feel the warmth of fresh blood. She felt as though she had torn through the fabric of a human's wares.

She opened her mouth, bewildered as the boar collapsed into a pile and deflated, his hide limp as though it were hollow.

She stood over it, growling but unsure of herself as something seemed to slither underneath the skin. A snake? No, it was too large for that. She stepped back.

Suddenly, from the claw marks she had left, out leapt a man. He was bloody and dirty, and he growled back at her.

She had never seen a trap like this before, but it was no matter. He was defenseless. She leapt atop him, sure she could kill him, but he did not fall.

Instead, she felt herself fall to her back on the ground as he pushed her down. He crouched over her, reaching closer.

She bit the man, her teeth sinking deep into his arm, but he still seemed not to care. Desperately, she swiped at him, her claws slashing across his skin. He bled, but the human would not die.

His hands circled around her throat and closed down. She could feel him crushing her windpipe. Her nostrils flared as she growled, losing breath. She scratched the man until she could see the bones in his arm, but still, he would not let go.

Her breath was running out as the sun

went black.

Her eyes flew open.

She was alone, completely and utterly alone. All she could hear was the dribbling from the nearby creek that dried up a little more each day. The sun was shining in the distance, and she could breathe easy.

She sighed into the bushes. Terror had found her again in her sleep. She hated when her dreams filled her with fear.

But nothing was near her as she woke, and it was only half a relief. There was nothing that could harm her, but there was nothing close to eat.

And she was still in the mountains. She hated being on the mountains, but it was far enough away from the cities to leave her safe from humans.

Still, she didn't dare leave her spot just yet. She stayed under the cover of the bushes as the sun began to set, shifting from her side to her belly.

If there was one good thing about the mountains, it was how the sunlight trickled over the mountaintops and loomed over it's sides at sunset.

She watched it intently, as she had every afternoon for the past few months. It glinted on the lake and shimmered in her pupils. She enjoyed it, staying perfectly still. She loved the last trickles of warmth against her fur as it sunk away from view.

As the sun disappeared, the stars came out of hiding in the dark of night. She stood from her spot and stretched out, feeling the weight in her toes. Her claws scraped against the soil.

She sauntered to the creek and crouched down to drink. Her tongue lapped into the water daintily, scooping up gulp after precious gulp to quench her thirst, hoping it could soften the hunger.

When she was done, she stood up and looked down into the creek. In the moonlight, she saw the tiger in the water. It's whiskers always twitched in time with hers.

It was the only other tiger she had seen for ages.

But she left it there again, walking down the creek to somewhere lower down the mountain, wherever there was something she could eat.

She had gone more days without eating than any time she could remember before, which left her hungrier than she had ever been.

She begged for a boar as big as the one in her dream to come before her now. She believed her stomach was empty enough that she could eat it whole.

2034

China

He didn't know if the blood on his hands belonged to himself or the tiger. His arm was still bleeding out, and the tiger was still on top of him, and the world was still turning even though the leaves had stopped falling midair.

He tried to push the tiger away, but it was unmoving like a stone, her eyes still transfixed on him. He could barely catch his breath, but it was enough to survive.

He may have still been alive, and the world beneath him may have still had a pulse, but the sky and the tiger and all that was above him were motionless, like a photograph. He did not know if he would ever escape.

He woke suddenly with a paw on his face and the sound of meowing.

He stared blankly at the cat, her face momentarily shielding him from the morning sun. She meowed again before stepping aside, letting it blind him.

He laid still, squinting as he let the morning sun seep in through the windows and onto his skin. Ahead of him came the sunshine reflecting from the driveway, and the road that lead to the city. Behind him lay the shade of the forest's edge, the protected trees leading from his backyard to the wild lands that still remained around the river. He wished that the shade of the trees could protect him now, to filter the light beaming directly onto his face.

Slowly, he sat up, his muscles sore and tired. The cat circled around him, meowing once more and rubbing herself against his arm. He knew she was hungry.

"Alright, Hu." He reassured the little cat, petting her across her back.

He stood up and Hu jumped down from the bed. Sensing that he was up, the lights in his room brightened, shining off of the white walls. He headed to the wall to the left of his bed, and faced the systems that controlled the cat's needs.

"Feed the cat." He ordered the house. A tube attached to a bag of cat food vacuumed up little bits of kibble to a holding section with a scale, which was attached to the wall. Once the right amount of food had been gathered, the vacuuming stopped, and it sent the kibble down another tube until the dry food tumbled down into her bowl. The cat immediately ran over to feast.

The man spoke again, "Give the cat fresh water." The bottom of the water dish gave way, sending the old water down the pipes, and then the bowl closed again. The long, thin pipe from the ceiling poured water into the dish until the bowl sensed that it was full.

The man gave another order, "Clean the litter box." The litter box whirred to life, the circular scooper filtering through the litter and picking up what was soiled. It poured a little more fresh litter into the box from the same kind of system that dispensed the food, but through a different track of tubes. It poured the used litter into a dark green plastic bag jutting out from the box's side. The machine pressed and sealed the used bag and a robotic arm picked it up and held it off to the side as another arm attached a fresh, empty bag to the side of the box.

He bent down to take the bag, his back aching as he straightened himself back up to stand. He couldn't imagine life without these modern conveniences, back when people had to scoop the litter themselves and pour out the cat food. It would leave him too sore. Bending over alone was a strain.

He turned right, towards the attached bathroom. He commanded, "Open the bathroom door." And the handle-free door sprung away into it's holding place between the walls.

He entered the bathroom, the lights coming on as he entered. He looked in the mirror at the wrinkles from decades of smiles and frowns, and his white, thinning hair. He disposed of the litter bag in the trash chute.

The cat continued to feast on the dry, meaty morsels, crunching them against her fangs. She ate until she was satisfied, and then drank, her tongue darting in and out of the water quickly, scooping in the water and swallowing it down.

She had nothing to worry about.

She walked into the bathroom where the old man was brushing his teeth, and meowed at him. He did not stop his brushing, so the cat rubbed herself against his leg, using only her head first, then leaning on him with all of her little body. She purred contentedly.

He spat out his mouthwash, then gave another order. "Retract sink." The sink was pulled back into the bottom half of the mirror, making it full-length.

The cat stared up at him. Despite knowing that it would send pain shooting down his back, he slowly bent down and reached for the cat. "Hu, I can't bend like this so much." He chided.

The cat stood on her hind legs to meet his hands. He chuckled, lifting her up to hold her. He scratched her behind her ears, and she gave him more purring.

She looked towards the mirror and meowed. She saw a mackerel tabby with brown fur and black stripes, the same cat Hu always saw reflected back at her. She reached out for it, one paw meeting the glass. She shifted in the man's arms, extending her other front paw to the mirror. Her back paws stretched, trying to stand on his hands, a back paw wavering near his wrist.

The old man chuckled. "Hu, I can't hold you when you're stretched out like this!"

It was true. The cat found herself falling out of the man's arms, but she landed gracefully on her feet.

She scurried alongside him as the lights in the bathroom faded off behind them.

"Open the bedroom door." He ordered. This door moved away the same as the bathroom door had done, and the cat bolted ahead. The lights in the big, open kitchen-living room came on. She headed straight for the catnip mouse on the floor, attacking it gleefully. She was focused on it as the man went to the stove and ordered it to heat up while he prepared a pot of broth to boil wheat noodles in for a soup.

She was a flurry of claws and teeth on the little cloth toy, not caring that she bumped into the sofa as she rolled around. She was lost in her assault as the man prepared his meal, but she perked up once he sat down at the sofa, his bowl and spoon in gloved hand.

"Turn on the television." He ordered the house. Moments later, the screen flickered on to the morning news. He pulled his spoon up from the soup, blowing before taking a taste of the savory meat and noodles.

The cat meowed, staring intently at the bowl.

"No, you just ate." The man said. She meowed again in response. He chuckled, shaking his head and plucking a floating noodle from the bowl. It dangled above the cat for a moment, but she captured the pasta and scarfed it down. He ate another spoonful himself as the anchorwoman on the television began a new story.

"A bit of better news today, the four thousandth Siberian tiger was born in the wild today. Released in an effort to repopulate the areas that were once home to it's close relative, the extinct Caspian Tiger, the Siberian tigers are thriving in—"

"It's not the same." The old man stated sadly.

The cat looked at him intently once more, but he did not look up from his bowl. He was as still as stone. His sorrow seemed to exude to the air around him.

He said it again. "It's good, but it's not the same."

1974

Turkey

The tigress had walked most of the night, but had found nothing. The moonlight illuminating the ground, usually so beautiful, instead was simply a light to reveal the deserted path ahead of her. Her impossibly heavy paws weighed her down as her head spun, feeling much too light. Her stomach ached, as it had for many days before, but worse. She could feel herself becoming sick from the emptiness.

She hoped for a deer, or at least a faun, though she was prepared to settle for field mice, as she had last time. But they were nowhere to be seen. She wondered if she could hunt out their burrows, even though she knew that mice would barely be enough. The mountains never provided for her.

She remembered when she lived in her home, back in the marshlands. She remembered hiding in the tall grass, crouching before chasing down her prey, and the splash of the cool, clear water beneath her paws as she ran. She remembered the deer and boars that would drink at the riverbank, and eating her fill of the unsuspecting prey. She remembered always having enough.

But the water got lower, and the creatures she once ate stopped coming to drink. That, or men found them first.

They may as well have eaten them all in front of her, so the tigers didn't have to wonder where the prey had gone for so long. And then the tigers dwindled. She remembered when the men starting hunting them down, she remembered how they would pour mysterious things into the stream and then all the tigers who drank from it would die. She knew the men wanted her dead, but she never new why. Nor did she know why they cleared the reeds from the marsh, leaving her no place to hide.

But, above the other tigers, she remembered her mate. She remembered the sun reflecting on the water so brightly that day they met. She had not expected to run into any other tigers when she went to drink, but he emerged from the few remaining reeds and walked up to her. She stared at him, taking in his scent, which was simultaneously foreign but deeply familiar, like a memory from a previous life. They left the water together, and for a week, they traveled the riverbank and hunted together.

She remembered the warmth of his body sleeping beside her during the cold nights, and the comfort she found in his bright amber eyes.

She remembered, a clear as a cloudless day, clearer than the riverbank she loved, the day they were walking by the water and the blast rang out. Something whizzed by in the air, it's wings swifter than a wasp, and it collided into her mate's side. Instantly, he dropped, splashing into the water. She knew he was dead— he didn't breathe, and the red of his blood flowed into the blue of the river. Still, she called for him, as if the sound of her voice would bring him back.

She didn't hear him stir. But she did

hear the click of the man reloading his weapon. Her eyes flicked towards the bushes, catching a flash of a silver rod.

She ran as fast as she could as she heard another loud crack. Somewhere behind her the killing thing flew by, but she kept running, her paws not slowed by the damp mud or the reeds or the splashing water. She ran until she could no longer see the body of her mate when she glanced back.

She remembered how it began her endless run from the men. She knew they had been after tigers, but it seemed that their numbers had gotten so slim that all the men were after her. She left the shrinking riverbank and the wonderfully open forest that was growing too thin and had to seek shelter in places she hated, anywhere that the men wouldn't find her. There were the too-dense forests that offered trees plentiful enough to cover the sight of her in exchange for also easily hiding her prey. And then, there were the mountains, like the one she had come to now. It was much too high for the boars and the deer, leaving her to eat injured birds and mountain goats.

She thought she might die to see another

goat— or, more likely, die *before* she found another. Even a beetle would do. Anything would be better than the painful, endless hunger that was weakening her body a little bit more with every passing moment.

Suddenly, her ears perked up. There was music in the air— a rustling, however tiny it might be, within the bushes.

The tiger ran, spending no time preparing, rushing to scarf down anything on the other side of the leaves. She nearly tripped on the dirt, but rebalanced, trampling over the bush with her mouth open and ready.

Though her fangs still dripped with saliva, when she laid her eyes upon the potential meal, she froze.

Laying behind the bush, small and wriggling, was a baby leopard.

She stood over the infant, breathing heavily. She couldn't remember the last time she'd seen a leopard, let alone a baby. It must not have been more than a couple days old, its eyes were still pressed shut. It yawned the tiny yawn of a kitten and licked its pink nose with an equally pink tongue. Any siblings it might have had were nowhere to be seen.

She knew she should eat the baby leopard. She felt the starvation ravaging her gut as she stared at it. She desperately needed to eat, she feared what would become of her if she didn't.

And yet, still, she stared at the little cub, feeling something very different than hunger. It mewed out, no doubt looking for its mother. It was much too young to be alone, but the tigress knew that the mother must be out hunting.

She knew, because she remembered her own cubs.

She remembered carrying her children within her alone as she continued hiding from the men. She remembered how she searched for a decent shelter far from the eyes of any humans as she could feel her pregnancy drawing closer and closer to an end. She eventually settled on a small cave on the outskirts of some more uncomfortably dense woods.

In that small cave, she gave birth to twins. It was a small litter, but she felt no disappointment, only joy. She could still hear their newborn squeaks. When they were old enough to open their eyes, she saw that they both had the same illuminated amber eyes as their father.

It was easy at first, when they only hungered for milk. When she needed to replenish herself, she would find something small in the nearby woods, and hurry back to keep her eye on the cubs. Their high-pitched mews for their mother were greeted by her own call, and their tiny, fuzzy bodies slept against her for warmth and safety. The world, for a few weeks, seemed to be a simple, beautiful place for the tigress.

But once they desired meat, it became more difficult. She searched farther and farther from the den, walking between more and more trees, hoping to come across something suitable for the three of them, like a faun. When she did, she would bring a part of it back to the den for the cubs and sleep soundly knowing they were still safe next to her. She was too afraid to bring them outside the cave on her hunts yet, lest they be spotted by human eyes.

Despite her efforts, they were found. She knew when she came back to the cave and heard silence instead of their usual mews.

Still, she dropped her goat carcass and rushed to the cubs, hoping she could stop what was already done, but knowing she could not. In a corner of the den they had known as their home, they lay motionless, their bodies cold to the touch of their mother's nose. Each one had a hole in them, the same kind of hole their father had received, but they seemed so much bigger on their little bodies.

Her cries and whimpers echoed through the little cave. She paced, knowing there was nothing she could do to save them, nothing to make her pain stop.

Until the sound of the shot. What flew collided with the cave wall, missing the tigress.

She turned, a loud growl leaving her throat. Her eyes met that of the man, and he trembled. She crouched and he stepped back, scrambling for something in his pocket and fumbling to put it into the open silver rod.

But she leapt onto him before he had the chance.

His screams filled the cave as he tried to push against her with his open, unloaded weapon, but it was no use. Her claws swiped against his chest and he cried out, flinching in pain just enough for her mouth to reach his neck. She felt the screams come out of his throat as she clamped down, teeth meeting warm, struggling flesh, and crunching through tiny human bones. He fell silent and still as his blood poured onto her tongue.

The memory made her all the more hungry as she gazed at the baby leopard. There was no sign of its mother anywhere nearby. She could swallow it whole, and no mother leopard would know to come after her.

But the infant's coos sounded so much like that of the tiger's own babies. She knew she couldn't bring herself to devour the cub.

The baby let out another mew, calling for it's absent mother. The noises from the tiger's still empty stomach almost overpowered the sound of the cries, but not quite. She wondered how hungry the leopard's mother was, and how long it would take for her to come back.

Though her own hunger still sent waves of pain through her weakening body, the tiger laid down next to the cub. The cub sniffed, knowing that the bigger cat smelled too strange to be its mother, but it rested it's tiny head on her fur anyway.

She laid with the cub as it drifted off to

sleep, but the tiger stayed awake. She searched for any leopard—or any man—that might approach. However, though the tiger kept watch all night, no one came.

2034

China

The old man felt lucky that he had finished his soup before the house began ringing. He knew it was his son's ringtone, but it didn't stop him from jumping whenever the house erupted with sound. The cat sat perched next to him on the sofa. He chuckled as he observed her looking around every direction at the ceiling, insatiably curious as to where the tone could be coming from.

Confirming again that it was his son, the system stated throughout the house, "Call from Yingjie."

"Answer phone on surround speaker

and surround mic." He ordered the house, not wanting to go back to his room to retrieve the smartphone.

"Hello?" He could hear his son's voice ask for him.

"Yes, hello, my boy!" He shouted.

He heard his son chuckle. "There's no need to shout, I can hear you."

"You know me. This new technology still confuses me sometimes."

A loud, shrill scream filled the house. "HI GRANDPA!" The cat meowed in annoyance as her fur stood up. The man could not help but laugh, the guffaws rolling out from his belly so loudly that he could barely hear his son scolding his granddaughter.

After a minute, he calmed down enough to say, "Oh, Meifeng, as your father said, there's no need to shout into the phone!"

"I'm sorry!" The little girl apologized.

The man assured her, "It's quite alright, my dear."

"Well, father, Meifeng and I were just wondering if we could drop by for a visit today."

"That would be wonderful." He said.

"Alright. We'll be over in about an hour. Hey, did you see the news this morning? About the tigers?"

"Oh, yes, I did."

"It reminded me of your tiger! Wasn't it one of them?"

The old man was silent for a long moment. The cat stared at him intently, letting out a small meow.

"Father?" His son questioned.

"Yes." The man answered finally. "Yes, she was a Caspian."

"Well, I was just wondering if I could show it to Meifeng." Yingjie asked.

"Oh, there's no need to show it to her, she wouldn't find it that interesting—"

"No, grandpa, I'd love to see the tiger!" The little girl chimed in.

The old man laughed, trying to hide his nervousness. "Mei, you realize the tiger's not alive, right?" The cat pressed her head against the old man's hand, demanding to be pet.

"That's okay, I still want to see it!" His granddaughter insisted.

He sighed. "Well, alright. You know how hard it is for me to say no to you."

"Yay! I get to see the tiger!" The child cheered. The man could hear his granddaughter's little shoes bouncing on the floor as she jumped up and down. His son chuckled at the girl's enthusiasm.

"We'll see you soon, father." His son said warmly.

"See you soon, Yingjie." He replied.

The house let out a soft, momentary tone to signify that his son had hung up the call. The man then let himself sigh. The cat, sitting next to him, stared up at him once more.

"I don't want to show her the tiger." He confided in the cat. She didn't make a sound in response, but stared back at him, craning her neck to look closer at him, as if to listen.

He sighed again, thinking the cat couldn't possibly understand him, and got up from the sofa. He took his bowl from the table to the sink and exited the room, the lights automatically fading behind him.

The cat followed him as he walked into his bathroom once more. He removed his clothes, and again the cat saw the decades-old, long, deep scar across the upper part of his right arm. She knew this scar very well.

"Turn on shower, medium-hot." The man ordered the house. The house dutifully turned on the shower, and in moments, the bathroom steamed up. He stepped in and pulled the curtain shut.

The cat remained sitting there, staring at the opaque shower curtain only momentarily before walking out of the room.

She jumped up onto the windowsill of the big window behind the sofa and looked out. At first, she saw only trees and the sunlight filtered through the leaves. But soon after, a bird flew up into a nearby tree and sat, it's tail flicking rhythmically as it sung. The cat's eyes widened and she crouched down. She chittered, wishing she could climb up the tree and catch the bird, wanting to taste a fresh kill, but she knew that she couldn't get through the glass.

Still, she stayed hyper focused on the bird, watching every flick of its tail and every hop across the branch. She tried to predict the bird's next move, tracking where it was looking, as if she could meet it wherever it went next.

The deliciously tense moments passed for her until the man walked up behind her, clad in his day clothes. "Watching the birds, little Hu?" He asked.

She gave no response. But the bird, spotting the man in the window, launched off of the branch and flew away somewhere above the trees. The cat's spell was broken, and she peeked around the forest floor before jumping down from the windowsill and walking off.

The man remained at the window, looking at the foliage, the forest floor, and all the places something could hide. "I wonder if I'll spot a tiger." He muttered, though he knew he wouldn't.

The cat jumped onto the sofa and looked back at him, wondering how long he would keep watching out the window when there were only trees to be seen. But, having grown tired from her little excitement, she turned away from him and laid on her side to take a nap.

1974

Turkey

The sun was rising when, in the distance, the tiger spotted an adult Anatolian leopard. The kitten stirred as the sun warmed her fur, yawning and stretching against the tiger's side. The tiger snorted, relieved. The hunger was only increasing every moment as she laid protecting the other cat's cub, but she couldn't bear to have left it alone without knowing it was back under it's mother's watchful eye.

The approaching leopard had been meandering slowly up the mountain path, but she froze as she spotted the tiger. It was only a moment's hesitation, and then the leopard mother ran, her teeth bared in a snarl.

The tiger stayed still, despite the charging leopard. It sped towards her, ready to give a killing blow, ready to seek vengeance for her cub.

She stopped in her tracks three feet in front of the tiger, when she saw her baby laying against her, still alive, still breathing.

Still, her teeth remain bared at the tiger. She growled and bellowed at the tiger, demanding that she leave, not trusting her or her act of kindness.

The tiger rose up slowly, careful not to frighten the angered mother, lest it lead to the leopard attacking. The cub sniffed the air and squealed, recognizing it's mother's presence.

The striped cat backed away from the kitten as the spotted cat came closer. Once the leopard deemed that the tiger was at a safe distance, the mother laid down next to her child to let it drink. Within moments, the baby was feeding.

She looked on at the peaceful mother and child that lay together in the sunrise. She was satisfied in knowing that the cub was safe.

But moments later, the tigress turned around and walked on down the mountain path.

She was deeply, almost dizzyingly tired. She knew she would usually sleep once it was daylight to avoid being spotted. But her hunger was too great to ignore, too sickening to sleep on.

She continued her hunt.

With each step that took her no closer to food, she felt that the mountains were forsaking her. She knew they would not provide for her as easily as any place she had hidden before, but she could almost feel the hunger killing her. Despite that sickening pang in her gut, she continued, knowing she had to go on if there was any hope of survival.

In the distance, she heard a bleat. Then another.

Her pace quickened as she went down the mountain, hearing what might be her salvation below. All at once, she was overjoyed to see that there were hundreds of sheep at the bottom of the mountain, but also stricken with dread when she saw the gates and the small house. She knew that at least one human dwelled there, and it surely wouldn't take kindly to her.

She knew the sound of their silver sticks and had seen them kill. She could only hope against her own better judgment that the ones who watched over this flock didn't have them.

Walking down the mountain, she traced over her plan. She could sneak into the pen and drag a sheep out, an old, sick one, or perhaps a lamb. If she bit it on the throat, she could effectively silence it. If she caught it by a leg, she'd have to quiet the animal by dragging it through the river just beyond the house, and then she could escape with her kill into the woods on the other side. She could see that the woods were too thick, too large for the men to properly track her down— at least, not before she caught them first.

She loved the feel of her paws on flat, low ground once more. Her claws could dig into the dirt and the blades of grass without hitting rock.

But she kept her body low to the ground, hoping to stay unnoticed. She crept towards the pen, the scent of the herd flooding her nose. She squeezed below the lowest wooden plank and into the pen, glancing for the weakest one.

However, she had made one vital mistake—in such a cramped space, her presence was easily noticed.

As soon as she reached the other side of the gate, her eyes met with the eyes of a sheep. It ran into the field of living wool, it's eyes going wide and it's fluff shifting as frantically as it's hooves as it screamed, alerting the others. They all scrambled away from her, to any other end of the pen, letting out their own screams to warn others and summon their caretaker. She could spot no weak link in their herd. She glanced at one sheep to another, trying to make a quick decision on which one to take.

But before she could strike, a man exited the house. He shouted out as he spotted her and ran back into his house, leaving the door wide open. She spotted the silver rod on his table before he could grab it.

She slipped back out of where she'd come in and ran across the side of the pen, panicking the sheep once more as they again ran to the side opposite of her, bodies crashing into the gate. The tiger ran from her salvation as quickly as she could. It seemed salvation had turned it's back on her.

She sprinted towards the river and

heard a terrible crack ring out somewhere behind her as she dove in. She swam desperately, barely peeking above the water.

She loved being in the water again, but couldn't take the moment to fully appreciate it as she escaped, her heart pounding loud enough for her to hear. Another shot was made, but it did not hit her.

She swiftly reached the other side and ran into the cover of the forest, then kept going, trees flying by her as she went deeper and deeper into the woods.

She stopped suddenly, deciding she was safe since there were no more blasts. She could hear the angered squirrels hiding in the treetops, and see the sun coming in through the leaves. She shook herself off, feeling water droplets fly off of her fur. She decided to lick herself clean rather than continue running damp. Her paws had already become unpleasantly muddy.

With every lick, she weighed her luck against her misfortune. Once more, she had escaped the men's killing things. But what does it mean to escape one killing thing if you fall to another?

She hoped to find a little bug curled between her toes, but she did not. Her hunt had once again spurned her, leaving her to continue the endless search. But, she did not resume the hunt until she had licked her fur relatively dry.

She began to walk through the trees again, through that accursed forest. She couldn't see anything moving beyond squirrels running too quickly up trees.

Her emptiness filled her with dread. She wondered if she would die in these woods. But she walked on, knowing that if she gave up her hunt now, then indeed, starvation would kill her.

2034

China

The cat woke up to the sound of the doorbell ringing. A tiny knock came at the door, too, and the cat knew at once who it was. She couldn't decide between feeling excitement or dread.

"Open front door." The man ordered as he stood up to greet his family.

The house complied to his order, and a little girl ran in ahead of her father. The child grasped onto the man's knees. "Grandpa!" She cheerfully cried out.

"My dear Meifeng, it's so good to see you

again!" The man greeted her warmly. It didn't take long before she let go of his leg and bolted towards the cat.

He looked at his son. He was the mirror image of the man's youthful self, though he always seemed taller each time the man saw him. He embraced his son. "Hello, Yingjie."

"Hello, father." His son replied warmly.

They were interrupted by an unhappy meow. They turned to see the little girl running towards them, her black pigtails bouncing as she carried the cat by her middle. The cat's tail curled up towards her stomach and her feet were extended out, claws drawn, but not striking. The cat's glare made her displeasure obvious, but she remained still and patient in the girl's arms.

"No, Meifeng, that's not how you hold kitties, remember?" Her father rushed over, taking the cat. He held the cat in his arms like a bundle, all her feet securely on an arm. "See, like this. Make your arms like this, and I'll give the kitty back."

The little girl put her arms together as instructed, and her father gingerly set the cat back into her hands. The cat sat pleased, closing her eyes and giving a small purr.

"See, she likes you!" The girl's grandfather said.

"Meifeing, speaking of cats, you wanted to see grandpa's tiger, right?" Yingjie asked.

"Yeah!" The girl agreed, still holding the cat.

The man chuckled nervously. "Oh, it's not that exciting. It's just the fur of a long dead animal, it's nothing to be worked up about—"

But Yingjie insisted, "Come on, father, I remember the tiger! I remember it's teeth, and your story, and how close a fight it was! It was always there when I was a child, I'd love for Meifeing to see it, too."

"I want to see the tiger, grandpa!" Meifeing nearly shouted, causing the cat to jump out of her hands. The cat ran up to the closed door on the wall opposite the entrance to the bedroom.

"Even Hu wants to see the tiger." Yingjie chuckled.

"Alright." The old man relented with a sigh, approaching the door. "I'll show you the tiger. This room is... full of my youthful transgressions. ...Open side room door." He ordered the house as the little girl cheered.

The cat bolted inside, and the little girl followed. She was immediately taken by the color, the dark wood lining the walls. On those walls, she noticed the heads of several deer, the tusk from an elephant, and a framed scale from the back of a pangolin. There was a desk with several notebooks setting on top of it, and in front of the desk lay a rug made from the fur of a tiger, it's arms spread, tail sprawled out, and head posed into an eternal snarl.

Meifeng stared at the tiger's face, at the polished teeth and the yellowish-amber glass eyes. Slowly, her grandfather came down to sit on the floor with her, both of them in front of the tiger pelt.

"This was a Caspian Tiger." Her grandfather said. "You see how bright the orange fur is, and how the stripes go black on the arms, head, and tail, but they're brown across the belly? And the stripes, see how they're thin, but close together? And the fur, feel the fur." He insisted. "Caspian's fur is so thick."

Meifeng pet along the tiger's back,

feeling it's lifeless fur under her fingers. The cat looked towards them and meowed.

"Tell her about how you killed the tiger!" Yingjie insisted enthusiastically. A silence hung in the room while the old man's eyes shifted to the floor. "I remember the story you used to tell, how you struggled but won against him—"

"Her." The old man spoke. "Caspians are one of the biggest tigers. But she was thin." He paused, his eyes watering. "She was starving."

"You never told me that." His son stated. But the old man gave no reply.

Instead, he continued his story. "I found her hunting far from where Caspians usually live. After she was dead, I was surprised at how light she was to carry. I know if she had been able to eat her fill, if she'd been at full strength, it would've been me instead of her." He hesitated, knowing the truth but hating to say it. "No one ever spoke of finding live Caspians after this one. She very well may have been the last." The old man wiped his eyes.

His granddaughter looked at him, her eyes wide, full of love and fear. "Don't cry, grandpa. There are still tigers at the river."

"None like this one." He said solemnly.

None of them spoke for a few more moments. The cat meowed, walking onto the tiger pelt. The old man chuckled. "You're such a strong girl, trying to comfort me. It's okay, Meifeng." He said as he hugged his granddaughter.

Yingjie chimed in, "Don't be so hard on yourself, father. This is how you took care of mother and me. You traveled around the world to hunt, you sold furs and scales and ivory, and you used the money to provide for us. And you brought back such thrilling stories! When I was young, you were such a great adventurer to me, and mother was always so happy when you came home."

Mother.

The man remembered her, the woman he called his wife. He remembered her shy smile, her unstoppable laugh, and the soft floral scent of her perfume.

He remembered her final days. She knew he was her caretaker, but she'd forgotten that he was her husband.

Hu was just a kitten back then, and she would take off running every time the woman shouted. Every time she wasn't allowed to do something by herself, her anger would come swift and loud, like a wild beast. But every time, he would accept her anger rather than risk her getting hurt.

He could handle her anger. It was her sadness that broke him.

On her last day, she sat and stared out the window. She was still waiting for her husband to come home. She did not recognize that he was there next to her.

"I'm tired of waiting for him to kill something. I wish he'd let them live, then he could stay with me." She said.

"But I'm here." He told her, not knowing if she understood him, not knowing if she believed him. He didn't see recognition in her eyes, only sorrow.

She wept for him, her husband in some distant land. Her husband held her and wept for her, still saying, "I'm here, you're not alone."

The next morning, he woke up to tiny, confused mews in his ear, from a kitten sitting where his wife should be.

Down the hallway, she laid motionless on the ground, like a rug.

He knew it was inevitable, but he expected that he would be there. He never wanted her to be alone when the end came, but fate was cruel. He didn't want to ask if it was instant or if it took time, but he hoped it was instant. He didn't want to imagine her alone and afraid as her life came to an end.

He didn't want to remember life coming to an end, alone and afraid, at the other side of his gun.

"Father?" His son asked, bringing him back to the present. Yingjie had a look of concern in his eyes, as though he were silently asking if he'd said something wrong.

The old man wiped his eyes from the moisture that had been forming again. He cleared his throat, and stated, "Well... I only wish I had chosen a different profession."

"When did you start feeling this way, father? It never seemed to bother you before."

"After your mother died, I started thinking about how precious life is, for every living thing. For her, and for us, but equally so for those creatures I killed." He paused once more. "Such a waste to kill for profit. This tiger only killed to eat."

His son reassured him, "Well, you didn't make a profit off of that tiger, father, you kept it!"

The old man sat there staring at the cat that his granddaughter was softly petting. The cat had curled up onto the tiger skin rug and rested her head atop the head of the tiger.

Finally, he said, "Worse still, I killed this tiger for pride."

Meifeing interrupted, giggling, "Grandpa, Hu thinks she's a tiger!"

The old man chuckled. "You know, there's one more thing I never told your father about this tiger. These eyes are wrong. Her eyes weren't entirely yellow. Around her pupils, they were green. The most vivid green I've ever seen."

"Oh, that sounds beautiful!" Yingjie remarked.

"She was." The old man agreed as he scratched his cat behind her ears. She closed her eyes and purred, her head still resting on the lifeless tiger.

1974

Turkey

There was the scent of a fresh carcass in the air. Salvation had returned.

She sniffed, following the scent like vultures would— in fact, she wouldn't be surprised if vultures were there, too. She had already ventured so far into the unfamiliar woods, and finally, finally, she would eat something. Anything. Thankfully, the closer she came to the source of the smell, the more she was sure that with such a strong scent, it had to be an animal of a decent size, something that was not simply a squirrel.

She could barely hear the thump of her

paws against the leaves and twigs on the forest floor as she maneuvered between standing trees and over fallen ones, her speed slowly increasing, hunger curling within her stomach and nauseating her, demanding to be satiated NOW. She wondered if it would take any time at all to devour the carcass.

She came upon it. Sweet salvation. A boar.

It wasn't the hairy, brown boar she was used to seeing— it was smoother, and pink. Not to mention, she couldn't tell what had killed it. It didn't have one of the holes from the silver rods, nor teeth marks. It had one long slit across its neck, and another long slit across its stomach, both of which had bled out. It made no sense for a fresh kill to be sitting out with nothing else eating it, but she was too hungry to question the miracle. The tiger inhaled the scent of the blood, savoring the stolen kill before she had even tasted it.

Her teeth sunk into the pig, and she found that it was still warm. The first bite went slowly as she let herself drink in all the flavors, the large bite hitting her empty stomach hard. All the other bites came in a ravenous flurry, the blood spreading across her mouth as she ripped the body apart and swallowed the life-saving meat down.

She could feel the headache gradually receding, the ever-looming threat of death lifting bite by bite. Surely, once this boar was done, it would last her long enough to find another substantial meal. By the time she finished this swine, surely the next time she hunted, she'd have the strength to kill.

A shot went through the air. Something flew by the tiger's ear, narrowly missing her and slamming into the pig. Blood poured out from the puncture.

She spun from the barely eaten carcass and saw the man. He looked different than the others she'd seen. He wasn't as light as the men who came to poison the river, but he was lighter than the men who lived around here. His eyes were narrower than either of theirs, and his hair was black. She had no time to speculate this as he was reloading the weapon. He had put something down the rods already.

He glanced up just as she leapt upon him, her roar almost loud enough to shake the earth itself.

His back slammed against the ground

beneath her, but he pressed the silver rod against her neck, holding her just out of reach. Her growls rumbled directly into the man's face as her fangs snapped towards him, hoping his hold would slip. But he stayed firm against her, her snapping teeth not meeting any flesh, only each other.

She lifted her mighty paw and slashed her claws across his right arm, digging into skin and flesh. He cried out as the blood came, and she lunged forward, inches from his nose, incredibly close to victory.

But the wild-eyed man pushed against her, and she felt her body rise, pushed backwards against the rod. She could see his sweat, his blood, his cringe from the obvious pain, and yet he still had the strength to push back against her.

Was he really that strong? Or had she become that weak? Her head pounded, still needing more of the pig to satisfy her hunger. She pressed back against the rod with all her might, but she could not move the man back down.

Against her strength, he managed to flip her over, her back hitting the ground as the man scrambled to his feet and backwards. The dizzying hunger shot through her once more and her eyes shut, almost involuntarily, as the world went hazy. She rolled over and stood, blinking until her vision was clear. The man, several feet away now, had clicked the stick back together. He pointed it straight at her.

With all the effort in her body, she gave another piercing, angry roar and leapt at the man, her fangs exposed, her claws out, ready to sink anything into him, desperate to kill him, desperate to eat, desperate to live.

Another blast rang through the forest, followed by complete silence.

The tiger landed on top of the man. The uncomfortably heated gun was pressed between him and the tiger. He could feel her blood trickle onto him.

He stayed still. The tiger's eyes stared unblinkingly into his. He kept his gaze on them, just in case the eyes moved. He stared long enough to see that in the tiger's yellow eyes, there was a band of a vibrant, brilliant green around her pupils. That is, her pupils that he was now sure were motionless. She fought no more. She moved no more. She breathed no more.

Once more, he pushed the tiger off of him. For a Caspian tiger, it was shockingly light. He could see her hipbones and some of her ribs beneath the fur, validation that he'd chosen the right trap to lure the hungry tiger to him.

As soon as she was off of him, he tended to his gashed arm. He peeled off his shirt and tied it tight against the top of his arm as a tourniquet. The blood flow thankfully slowed down, but he knew it would leave a scar, one that would last the rest of his life, if he was lucky enough to keep the arm.

He knew he had to act quickly to get the medical help he needed. He awkwardly shoved his unloaded gun through his belt, and grabbed the tiger by the back legs. As quickly as he could, he pulled the lightweight tiger through the woods, going towards the grassy path where he knew his colleagues were waiting by the truck.

They had said he was full of himself when he said he'd kill a tiger on his own, but now he would show them. Even if they still thought he was an idiot for going alone. Even if they were angry because he came within inches of death for it.

He thought about the tiger he dragged through the dirt and decided, since it had almost killed him, and since it was the first Caspian he'd seen in quite some years, that he wouldn't sell this one. He'd keep it as a trophy. In fact, he could picture it making a very nice rug.

2034

China

"Goodbye, grandpa!" Meifeing waved goodbye out of the window of her father's car.

Her grandfather waved back, smiling. Yingjie waved his hand out the window too, then backed his car out of the driveway and maneuvered onto the road. The old man was alone again.

He turned around, trying not to look into the sun, instead looking towards the trees leading to the forest behind his house. He wondered how far away the nearest tiger was. In one of the windows of his house, he could see the cat sitting and staring at him from behind the glass.

He slowly walked back to the house. At the front door, he put his hand against the surface and it illuminated, scanning his fingerprints. The system verified that it was him and opened the door, swiftly closing behind him once he was inside.

The cat meowed, greeting him. He stared at her for a moment, unsure what to do. He had avoided entering that room for so long. Now that he had, he felt drained somehow. He had stayed away from it long enough that he'd forgotten the actual size of the pangolin scale and the exact expressions of the deer on the wall, but he never forgot the tiger's face.

He walked towards the room, intending to order the door shut, but paused, and decided instead to walk in. The cat followed in behind him.

He looked around once more at the spoils of his past. He didn't want to remember killing all the things in the room, but he did, the tiger clearer than any other.

He walked over to the desk and sat down behind it. The journals of what he had done sat in front of him, a different book for each year.

The cat jumped onto the desk, slinking around the books and sitting in an available space near the desk's edge.

He went through the stacks until he pulled out the volume labeled 1974.

He opened it, flipping through, looking for the word 'Caspian tiger' until he fell upon it. He chuckled, and said to the cat, "Arrogant young me. All I wrote was, 'Killed Caspian tiger by myself. It scratched my arm pretty good.' Didn't mention I almost died. Didn't even mention how thin it was. Didn't say it might have been the last one."

He sighed, feeling sweat starting to come off of his forehead. He ordered, "Open windows." The glass was pulled upwards into a housing inside the wall, and a breeze came in. He sighed, not feeling much better, and noticed the date.

He knew he'd killed the tiger sixty years ago, but he didn't realize it had been sixty years to the day.

He set down the open book, a sadness coming over him. His elbow met the table, and his mouth went to his hand.

He could still see the tiger eating the pig.

He knew it was starving when he saw it. He almost didn't shoot out of pity, but he had to prove to himself that he could take down a tiger alone, even if it was a weak one.

He could still see the tiger's motionless eyes bearing into his own. He still felt it's body on him, light in weight, but heavy in it's own way.

The old man wept quietly, consumed by regret. He looked at the rug, knowing he would never see a living one again. Hu stared at the man, making no sound.

He was still sweating and upset when, suddenly, there was a pain in his left arm, as sharp as a knife. It instantly spread to his heart.

He gasped, clutching his chest. He stood from the desk and took a few steps to its side. He shouted, "Call an ambulance!" Just before falling on his side. A few feet in front of him was the snarling face of the tiger skin rug.

"What is your emergency?" The automated voice of the house asked.

Though his voice was hoarse, he managed, "Heart.... Heart..."

The house gave a ping, then confirmed,

"Requesting ambulance for heart attack."

He wheezed, knowing the hospital wasn't far, but not knowing if the ambulance would come on time. His wheezes came unsteady and pained as he stared at the angry animal in front of him. Hu still sat on top of the desk, looking down at the old man.

The cat had always known that his final breath would belong to her, just as hers had belonged to him. She had always thought she'd rip his eyes out, or re-open that old scar. This was the chance she had been waiting for all along. Even doing nothing, just watching him die alone and afraid while looking at what she once was, might be vengeance enough.

But now that her moment was here, she didn't feel like she thought she would at all. She thought his death would exhilarate her, but instead, she felt an odd sadness. Even if she did nothing, his dying thoughts would be of her.

She jumped down from the desk, and looked into the man's face as he shed frightened tears. She could feel his labored breaths reaching through her fur.

She walked into the old man's line of sight and sat down on all fours, positioned in front of the tiger. She meowed.

He wheezed, "Hu." She meowed back, sniffing upwards towards him, as she would when she wanted to be pet.

He reached towards her, his hand meeting her small back, and petted her soft fur. The man's breathing quieted down, though it was slowing.

He stared into the cat's eyes, unsure what he was looking for. Her yellow eyes stared straight back at him. Until he noticed something he'd seen many times before, but only now understood. Around her pupils was a band of brilliant green. It was like looking into the eyes of an old friend, one who'd changed over the years but still remained the same.

He softly chuckled, and a smile broke over his face. Knowingly, he whispered, "Little tiger."

His final breath was calm, steady, and unafraid.

Hu remained still. She expected to be comforted, but she wasn't. All she felt was loss— the weight of his death, her own death, and the suffering between them, all the suffering that never needed to exist. She thought she could destroy man like man destroyed her, but it seemed that man eventually destroys itself.

Finally, she stood up, leaving the body behind her and facing the open window. She had to continue, there was no other option. It's what she always did, how she always survived. She had to keep going.

She jumped up onto the windowsill, looking out into the trees. She took a moment to look back, at the dead man and the rug and the room full of death, then looked back out to the world, and jumped down to it.

She landed on her paws onto the dry dirt below. Her claws sunk into the soil, feeling nature between her toes for the first time since a previous life. She walked on, paws hitting soft grass. She took in the scent of the grass, fresher than anything from inside the safety of the house she'd lived in. She could hear sirens behind her, arriving at the house too late, as she went between the trees.

She walked on for a long time. All the trees felt bigger than ever before. Even the dense forest she was in seemed to have all the room in the world. Her ears perked up when she heard a distant stream.

She ran for the water, her feet crunching against fallen leaves. It had been so long since she'd seen a river.

She came upon the clear water and froze. A short distance away, a field mouse was drinking. She darted to the nearest fallen tree, unnoticed by the mouse.

She sat perched and hidden behind the log, taking quiet breaths, waiting patiently for the right moment to strike the mouse. He drank from the stream silently, so quiet that not even the ears of a cat could pick up on it.

He was still unaware of her presence, which made him the perfect prey— an easy, quick kill, dead before it could scream. Her mouth was already watering at the mere thought of his flesh, a fresh kill, for the first time in so long.

She dug her paws into the dry soil, ready to attack. A leaf crackled below her.

The mouse looked up suddenly, staring towards her. She stayed perfectly still and silent, her nerves on edge. She couldn't be noticed now. Not now.

Still, he stared her way. She didn't know if he could see her through the log, or if he knew purely off of her misstep.

The mouse turned and ran.

She leapt over the fallen tree and ran for the mouse. He was scurrying for a home tree, but she ran faster than he could. Her teeth sunk into the mouse's body. His tiny squeaks and screams rang out.

He couldn't escape her, though he thrashed against her. Her teeth dug into him further, tasting his hot blood, and he went limp. His body was her feast.

She devoured the field mouse ravenously. She did not expect to get so full from a mouse, but again, she'd forgotten how small she was now.

Her stomach full, she turned back towards the river. She came to the cool, clear water, and hunkered down to drink. Her tongue darted in and out of the water, and she decided that she liked it, even if it wasn't her river. It wasn't the same, but it was good.

When her thirst was satisfied, she stood and looked at the river. After a moment of considering, she began to walk the direction the river flowed from. She knew it probably wasn't the right stream, but she decided she would follow it, and she would keep going until the next river, and the next one, until she found the right one.

She was sure that if she kept going, she'd eventually find the other tigers.

THE LAST CASPIAN TIGER

Author's Note

The Last Caspian Tiger was always going to be an emotional project, I knew that from the start, but it's important to remember that this isn't a story of forgiveness. This story is about suffering, empathy, mercy, and perseverance. While life has it's share of good times, there are also the times that you find yourself suffering. Sometimes it's a familiar suffering, but other times it seems incredible, perhaps it's even tempting to call it unimaginable, but given enough thought, you can find the ability to see yourself in anyone's place. This is the importance of both empathy and mercy. When you recognize that someone is suffering, you shouldn't make an effort to make it worse— that is, you don't want to become the man who shoots a starving tiger. Likewise, when someone tries to strike you down, you must defend yourself, you have to fight for your life and everything you know that's worth protecting. I say this story isn't about forgiveness because some things are unforgiveable. The tiger comforts the man in his death not out of forgiveness, but because she recognizes his suffering, just as he has come to recognize the value of life in the animals he killed, as well as the suffering he caused. The tiger offers the man the comfort and mercy that he regrets denying her. It's not about forgiveness, it's about the pain they have in common. Finally, perseverance, in the face of everything. To continue living and fighting, even when it seems hopeless. No matter what happens to her, the tiger always continues, she never stops. No matter what, you have to find your way.

Speaking of continuing, this story began as a failed NaNoWriMo project. I began it one November and didn't finish it, and set it aside for a year while I concentrated on another writing project that I hope to publish soon. I'm very glad that I picked this short story back up and that you're reading it now.

It's funny because when you have a story that you've started, it never leaves your mind, and next thing you know you start seeing tigers everywhere you go. Of course, there are the tigers you purposely put in front of yourself, like the tiger I set as my desktop photo that November and is still my desktop photo right now, reminding me to finish this thing I started. But, it's different when they start popping up everywhere. Everybody starts having tigers on their jackets, this guy who works with big cats goes viral, Kesha goes on tour and her poster has a tiger growling on it and so do the concert t-shirts and then she tattoos a tiger to her hand...

Kesha motivated me a lot while I was writing this, both as a person and as a writer. Her most recent album *Rainbow* is incredibly moving and meaningful. She fights, she lives, she continues. It makes sense to me that she surrounded herself with tigers, because she is one, in many ways.

Another influence I have to mention is the Megadeth song "Countdown To Extinction", from the album of the same name. In a lot of ways, it was the perfect song to help me get into the mood required to write about what humans have done to tigers; the lyrics were extremely relevant, both angry and sad.

Then, of course, there's my cat. I dedicated this book to her because, as I said, this idea wouldn't have happened without her. I can't count all the times I've looked at her and thought that she was probably a wild animal in a recent past life.

Thank you for reading my book! If this story moved you, I implore you to consider donating to the World Wildlife Fund or the

Wildlife Conservation Society or a similar charity to help with the conservation of tigers and their habitats. The number of tigers is thankfully increasing, but they still need your help to keep it going up.

Zoe Jazz

ABOUT THE AUTHOR

Zoe Jazz is the Creative Director at Semi-Permanent Press. She grew up and lives in Orlando, Florida. The Last Caspian Tiger is Zoe's first publication.

Look for news on her website: www.jazzhandthatwrites.com

www.SemiPermanentPress.com